THE SILENT JOURNEY

PRAKHAR GUPTA

Contents

Preface

The Silent Journey
Through hard work, sacrifice, and commitment, an extraordinary fictional scientist devoted his life to space, inspiring us all to pursue our passions with unwavering dedication.

ONE

INTRODUCTION

It was nearly 6:00 p.m. in Bengaluru, India, and the press conference was about to begin. A large group of news reporters had gathered to interview a scientist, and I was among them. It was my first time seeing such a large crowd waiting to speak with a scientist, and I didn't know much about this particular scientist.

As I was lost in thought, a person walked into the hall and everyone stood up. I later found out that it was the scientist, Sagar Yadav. He went up on stage and began addressing the crowd. Suddenly, there was a loud noise as Sagar Yadav collapsed onto the stage before he could complete his speech. He was soon hurried to the hospital.

Enter Caption

As I reached my home, I couldn't shake off the thoughts of the scientist from my mind. This was a first for me in my career that spanned almost 20 years. The next morning, I hurried to the hospital where Sagar was admitted after having suffered a heart attack. Although I couldn't meet him, I did meet his close friend, Vishal. I convinced Vishal to talk about Sagar and we went to a nearby room to discuss his life.

Vishal said, "The people who break social barriers are often not well-known." This sentence made me curious about the life story of Sagar Yadav. I don't remember exactly what Vishal said, but his story about Sagar always touches my heart whenever I hear it.

Vishal said:

The life story of Sagar Yadav, who could have been a well-known scientist, is known by only a few due to his non-famous status for breaking the barriers of society.

Sagar was born into an impoverished family in a small village in Eastern Uttar Pradesh. Unfortunately, the village he was born in judged people based on their caste and income. His father was a landless laborer and his mother was also forced to work in the fields for a meager income. They were expecting their fifth child when Sagar was born. Sadly, he lost his two elder brothers before he was even born. Growing up, Sagar had to live in a very dirty place and often crawled in muddy water. Despite losing her two sons to infections caused by these conditions, Sagar's mother was forced to let him live in the same conditions. Sagar used to play with his two siblings, a sister, and a 7-year-old brother.

Sagar was quite different from his siblings. Even at the age of eight, he loved reading books. He would go to a nearby scrap dealer, clean up the area, and receive a book in return. This went on for a year. Soon, Sagar's father realized his son's interest in studies and began thinking about sending him to school. His father had never considered sending any of his children to school before, as he never imagined being able to afford the fees. Sagar's siblings also never attended school and would wander around while Sagar read his books.

Sagar's childhood conditions surely reminded me of my childhood but his was even tougher. I was filled with sympathy for him. Soon we realized that the doctors were rushing outside our room into Sagar's operation theatre. On further inquiry, we learned that Sagar was in serious condition. I was almost crying after seeing his condition.

I even saw years in Vishal's eyes and I consoled him and myself as well. The nurse told us that these kind of operations takes hours to complete and are generally successful. It made us calm and we needed this kind of assurance.

TWO
EARLY DAYS

After we received consolation from the nurse, Vishal began the next part of our story. I braced myself for more sorrow.

'Sagar was not only very good in studies but was very humble and kind as well. I still remember how he used to give away his food to stray dogs even when he was hungry for hours'. His family couldn't even arrange two square meals a day during a part of the year.

Sagar never complained to his parents about poverty or hunger like his siblings. At age 10, his father finally decided to take him to a nearby school. Sagar's father took him directly to the headmaster's office where Sagar was asked a few questions by the headmaster. Soon Sagar's father asked him to wait outside the room. While Sagar was waiting outside, he heard a noise from a nearby class. Sagar went inside and found a teacher teaching Maths to 7th graders. He soon saw a question on the board that no one could solve. Sagar didn't hesitate to take the chalk from the teacher and solve the question. Very soon the question was complete. It left the students and the teacher wondering how a 10-year-old solved a 7th-grader question without prior education.

Before anything could be asked a noise came from the headmaster's room. He was shouting at Sagar's father to get out. Sagar and his father were forced to leave the school. Later Sagar found out that his father was asking for fee waivers for Sagar but the headmaster denied it. Sagar cried that night as he understood that he would never be able to go to a school in his life. Even Sagar's father was heartbroken.

The next day, Sagar was going to the scrap dealer to get more books soon he saw a man approaching him. It was that teacher who was impressed by the knowledge of Sagar. Firstly, Sagar was amazed but prepared himself for further humiliation.

To his surprise, the teacher asked to meet Sagar's parents. He then asked Sagar 'Would you like to go to school?'. Sagar was confused in the beginning but said stuttering 'Yes'. Then the teacher introduced himself as Deepak. He belonged to a middle-class family and was teaching at that school for about 12 years. He said that he was amazed when he saw Sagar solving such questions at such an age. Sagar then explained about how he managed to get such knowledge.

Then, after a long discussion the teacher, Deepak gave an offer to Sagar. Deepak told Sagar that he would pay Sagar's school fees but in return asked for Sagar's hard work, to which Sagar happily agreed. Even Sagar's parents were overjoyed as Sagar was the first one who would be going to school in their entire family.

Soon Sagar was admitted to the 7th class, he was the smallest by age in his entire batch. It was not very easy for Sagar to make new friends there. Many students jokingly called him poor and made fun of Sagar's poverty but these humiliations turned out to be a motivation for Sagar. Sagar used to study very hard and even his parents supported him. His siblings were quite jealous of him and started almost hating him immediately. When he used to get a lot of disturbance from his house he would go to a nearby park and study under the lamp. Sagar understood very soon that a very tough life awaited him ahead his dreams would be shattered multiple times before reaching the abode of clouds.

Enter Caption

THREE
NEW BEGINNINGS

Time soon passed and as promised Sagar kept on working hard. He used to go and meet Deepak every 2 days. Deepak started tutoring and mentoring Sagar. Very soon the results of the 7th class were out. Sagar not only was the top scorer in his class but also of the entire batch. He scored an impressive 99% shocking everyone.

The world seemed to have completely changed for Sagar but he was concerned about one thing only and that was his siblings. Sagar tried to teach them many times what he learned in school but they were not at all interested in studies. His siblings even started to disturb him many times while he was studying but it had no impact on his studies.

He worked hard, passed his 10th class, and was the highest scorer in his district. His village lacked a senior secondary school, forcing him to study in the nearby city, Gorakhpur. First of all, Sagar was doubtful whether his parents would allow him to go and study too far for his further studies. At last, Sagar finally decided to ask his parents to which his father agreed and replied to his hesitant mother "Your children are not your children. They are the sons and daughters of Life's longing for itself. They come through you but not from you. You may give them your love but not your thoughts. For they have their thoughts."

Deepak and Sagar then left for Gorakhpur the next day. Deepak helped Sagar in searching for a good school and accommodation. Very soon Sagar adjusted himself to his surroundings and worked his level best. In those two years, he won many Olympiads and national-level competitions. Things seemed to change for him a lot.

He was very good in subjects like Physics and Maths and also had a scientific temperament. Despite such a good academic career he every day used to remember the conditions in which his family was living and every day dreamt to bring his family out of poverty.

While studying he also developed his skills in aircraft and rockets. He always used to admire an airplane while in the sky and developed his interest in the field of aeronautical engineering.

His consistent dedication and hard work once again paid him with excellent rewards. He scored extremely high in class 11th and did wonders in class 12th by scoring the highest marks in his entire state, Uttar Pradesh. His parents were overjoyed and so was he.

FOUR
TROUBLE BEGINS

Little did he know that the trouble in finding a college wouldn't be that easy. He applied to several colleges for his dream to become an aeronautical engineer. Even his teacher, Deepak was helping him and Deepak secretly decided to apply to Harvard University for Sagar.

Firstly, Deepak was not very confident about Sagar's admission to Harvard so he kept on searching for good colleges for Sagar. In this pursuit one day a postman delivered a letter at Deepak's house. It was from Harvard.

Deepak shivered while opening the letter but became overjoyed upon reading it. Harvard had granted admission to Sagar and that too with hefty scholarships.

Enter Caption

Deepak was overjoyed and confused at the same time. He didn't know how he would convince Sagar to study in a faraway land for 4 straight years. At night finally, Deepak decided to talk to Sagar, at first Sagar denied the offer as he wasn't ready to go too far.

Confused Deepak was somehow able to convince Sagar's parents by telling them the importance of such a college. Sagar continued his negligence. Finally, Sagar's mother went to Sagar's room at night and told him about the struggles that she faced due to poverty and also told Sagar how he has an opportunity today to change their future. Somehow Sagar was convinced and his passport and visa procedures were started.

He left for the U.S.A. the next month all alone. He knew that the troubles in his life had just begun and the journey had just started. He had only about ?1000 in his pocket which was close to $12. He didn't know where and how to go in that unfamiliar land. A feeling of nervousness struck him as soon as he boarded his flight. Probably he was traveling by airplane for the first time that too all alone.

He somehow managed to reach Harvard without taking a cab. He was desperately searching for a room to stay and searched for it nearby. Soon Sagar met me, Vishal. He rented a room which was just beside me. Both of us introduced ourselves and I still remember when Sagar first saw me he was overjoyed to see an Indian next door.

As the story was being continued another rush of doctors was to be seen outside. I and Vishal were still worried about Sagar's condition and were praying. I too got attached to Sagar although I never met him. For the first time, I became very informal in a case. I took interviews about many crime incidents, and accidents even from many celebrities, but Sagar's case probably became an exception.

Shortly after our arrival, a doctor approached us with the news that Sagar was in critical condition. He informed us that if Sagar didn't regain consciousness within the next 24 hours, we might lose him. Although this news was extremely distressing, we decided to continue with our story. As I pondered on the story, an important question occurred to me: why do the lives of scientists go unnoticed? This question reminded me of a case that occurred three months prior, where a famous film star lay on his deathbed. The media was stationed outside his hospital room and updates on his condition were broadcasted for around four to five days. This news was the topic of discussion in every coffee shop for about a month. Although he was a hero in movies, why do we forget to celebrate real heroes like Sagar? His inspiring story went unheard and his personal life never received any media attention, until now.

Vishal then washed his face and returned to the conference room. He was nearly crying but on seeing my curiosity for Sagar he started again. He started by saying- "When your time is bad then nothing works" he said that Sagar was short on money and had rented a room without even getting a part-time job. Sagar slept hungry on the first day itself in a faraway land. The next day he shamelessly came to me and asked me if I had any work for which I could be paid. I belonged to quite a poor family, and as a result, I worked at a nearby café. I assured Sagar that I would help him get employed there. The café owner was quite strict and offered meager wages to Sagar. To my surprise, Sagar agreed to do such hard work.

Every day I saw Sagar work for hours and I used to feel sorry for him many times. I used to see Sagar's cottage photo whenever I visited Sagar's room. When I asked about this to Sagar he would reply by saying that this image reminded him why he came so far. He used to add that he had just one dream and that is to abolish his family's poverty. That day the spark that I saw in Sagar's eyes made me rethink my ambitions.

FIVE

Path Ahead

Enter Caption

Classes started soon and my friends and I used to attend parties frequently. However, Sagar was different. He never joined us at any of these parties, despite money not being an issue. We would often offer to pay for him, but he never agreed.

He used to wake up at 4:00 a.m. daily and work towards his goals. Our four years passed quickly. While Sagar worked 14-16 hours a day, I spent my time partying.

We observed similar outcomes in the job hunt. Sagar landed a lucrative position at NASA, whereas I was still on the lookout for one. I vividly recall how ecstatic Sagar was when he informed his parents about his job at NASA, and their reaction was priceless.

Sagar was thrilled about his first job and decided to go straight to Washington D.C. without returning to India, feeling on top of the world.

I also got a job in a not-very well-known firm. Despite being quite successful Sagar never forgot his friends. He used to contact them both in India and the U.S.A. frequently.

"He started working in a junior position and his hard work paid off quickly. In just a few years, he was promoted to head of communications at NASA. He was so excited about his success that he went back to his hometown to share the news with his family. I went with Sagar and was shocked to see the poor living conditions his family was enduring."

They had a tiny cottage and could barely manage 2 square meals a day. Sagar's sole purpose for returning to India was this only. He bought a new house and kept a maid to support his family. I felt satisfied after seeing their conditions improve.

Next year, even bigger news came. Sagar got to lead a Mars mission. I still remember how we celebrated that achievement. It was a 2 year long mission. Sagar gave his everything in this mission.

Sagar was working hard for this mission but bad news soon struck him. His parents and siblings were going on a bus when the bus fell from the mountain leaving all passengers dead. This tragedy disheartened Sagar. Even I felt the pain that Sagar was going through. Still, there were six months left for the Mars mission. Sagar decided to go back to his hometown for at least a month.

I heard from Sagar that he met his teacher, Deepak there who suggested to him never to give up no matter what. I don't know how deeply Sagar took Deepak's words but Sagar was surely affected by this tragedy. Deepak also understood that the tragedy of losing his entire family affected Sagar mentally. Sagar would roam here and there in India and indeed the tragedy of losing his whole family disheartened Sagar.

Finally. when I heard about Sagar's bad conditions, I went back to India and brought him back to the U.S.A. I could only imagine his condition during that time.

SIX

SORROWS

Sagar trudged to the office, his heart heavy with a crushing weight of disappointment and sadness. Despite his struggles, he was determined to keep working. However, he found it difficult to maintain his focus and drive, and his work began to suffer as a result. Sagar knew he needed to find a way to lift the weight from his heart and regain his motivation, but it was easier said than done.

While the most awaited satellite was being launched towards Mars, I(Vishal) watched closely as Sagar led the mission.

One fine day, when everything seemed to be going well, I was getting ready for work when some shocking news reached me. The satellite that NASA had sent to Mars had lost its communication in the morning. The whole country was in mourning. Strangely, Sagar was blamed for the failure of the mission. Sagar's name became the headline news and he was held responsible for the unsuccessful mission. Despite his attempts to convince his seniors that it was the team's fault, not his alone, no one listened to him.

Enter Caption

Depressed Sagar had to leave his job. I still remember the tears that went down his face as he decided to resign from his position. It was not easy for Sagar as he lost both his family and job within just 8 months.

Sagar went through a difficult period, likely the worst of his life. I tried to encourage him to move on and search for a new job, but unfortunately, his name and reputation had been ruined by the media, making it difficult for him to find employment. This went on for about six months, but luckily, Sagar had enough savings to cover his expenses for at least a year more.

Sagar was already heartbroken when he received another devastating news. His childhood teacher, Deepak, who had helped him in the past, was hospitalized with a serious condition. Sagar immediately rushed back to India to be by his teacher's side.

Upon Sagar's arrival in India, he was in disbelief about what was happening in his life. Fortunately, Sagar reached India just in time to see Deepak, who was on his deathbed. Despite his condition, Deepak offered one line of advice to Sagar that would change his life forever. Deepak already knew about the struggles in Sagar's life and said, "Never give up in your life, no matter what," before passing away.

SEVEN

THE STRUGGLE

As evening approached, Vishal and I were discussing the story when we noticed a commotion outside the conference room. A group of doctors informed us that Sagar had finally regained consciousness. We were delighted to hear the news and rushed to see him. Sagar's story deeply touched my heart and I was curious to learn more about how a scientist who had lost everything could rebuild his life. The sunset from the conference room added to the emotional moment.

I was also soon called by Vishal to meet Sagar. I was introduced as a curious reporter to Sagar. Sagar was also quite interested in me.

Sagar finally continued the story the next morning. He began by saying, "When God closes one door, he opens another one. You should continue to search for it." He mentioned that it was undoubtedly a difficult period for him, but he recalled Deepak's final words and resolved to give it another shot.

Then, upon seeing Sagar's condition deteriorate once again, Vishal decided to continue the story. He began with, "The very next day, he went to Bengaluru to apply for a job at the Indian Space Agency, the most famous agency in India. He had confidence in his mind but doubt in his heart.

He said with a smile that convincing the directors at ISA to give him a job was a tough task. They were reluctant to give him such a high position even when he had made a blunder just a few months ago. Sagar's confidence impressed the directors and was selected to lead a Mars mission for his country. This decision was based on Sagar's extensive experience with challenging missions, which made him one of the most qualified individuals in the country for the role.

This time, Sagar was determined to give it his all. However, things were different this time. Unlike NASA, he had limited time and resources to accomplish the mission. He often slept in his cabin at night to avoid wasting time in traveling.

EIGHT

A COMEBACK IS BETTER THAN A SETBACK

Sagar spared no effort to ensure the success of this mission. Despite facing criticism for his previous mission, he persevered with determination.

Time passed quickly, and the day of the rocket launch was approaching. I vividly remember when Sagar got a high fever just a week before the launch. Despite his illness, he insisted on going to work. When I tried to stop him, he simply said, "Work is the priority; everything else can wait."

I anxiously kept my fingers crossed until the rocket finally reached Mars' orbit after an 8-month journey. Each day was filled with stress for both Sagar and me. I was aware that another mistake could damage Sagar's reputation. Sagar also knew it was his last chance to prove his worth.

Enter Caption

On the final day of the epic mission, I vividly recall Sagar gazing at the sunrise upon waking. Sagar was both tense and determined on the final day.

Even I was praying the entire day. In the afternoon, around 1:00 p.m., I finally received the news I had been waiting for years. The Mars mission led by Sagar was a success. The news just had one thing to show: "Sagar did it, India is on Mars." I was overjoyed too.

I still remember the moments when I congratulated him and said, "You did it." and he replied by saying, "We did it."

Even Sagar got a call from NASA requesting him to join back but Sagar had already made a tough decision.

NINE

DESTINY LIES BEYOND

I remember the moment vividly. We were still in the hospital meeting room, and Sagar was resting in his bed. Just as I thought the inspiring story had come to an end and was about to get up from my seat, Vishal said, "But."

I was stunned when Vishal said, "Sagar had finally regained his lost glory, but now he wishes to make some big decisions in his life." It took me a while to recover from this shock as I wondered what important decision he was going to announce at the press conference.

Vishal initially refused to disclose the decision, but after I insisted, he instructed me to attend the press conference hosted by Sagar the next day.

I returned home to a surprising discovery. I couldn't fathom what decision Sagar would announce at the press conference the next day.

Finally, after a long night, I prepared myself to attend the press conference, likely dressed in my best attire. Still unable to imagine the decision he was about to make. Would he rejoin NASA or announce his retirement? These thoughts were already causing my blood pressure to drop.

Finally, Sagar took the stage, heightening my anxiety as I braced for an unexpected response. He started by saying "Today, I have reached this point with the support of many people. However, in this journey, I forgot my original purpose. Although I may have made a difference in the country, I have not been able to bring about significant change in my hometown of Uttar Pradesh. There is still inequality that needs to be addressed. As a result, I have decided to return to my hometown and establish a school that is free from all kinds of inequalities. This school will not only provide quality education but will also inspire lower castes to pursue their goals, just as I did, even if it means breaking social barriers."

I was dumbstruck as I never expected such a response. After achieving so much, he still wants to go back to where he started. I was inspired by the humbleness of Sagar and realized that it would be the best for Sagar.

Time passed quickly, and after a year, I finally decided to meet Sagar in his hometown. I went to Uttar Pradesh and was astonished to see a massive building just near the railway station. Sagar named the school after Deepak, the teacher who helped him a lot. I saw the perfect example of diversity and equality there. Such a school was hard to find even in cities at that time, but he managed to create one in his village. The school had affordable fees and an excellent staff. That day, I realized that one person can have the courage to change the mindset of an entire society.

His story motivated me to write about him as many inspiring stories of individuals often go unnoticed, prompting me to write this book to bring their silent journeys into the limelight. I began with Sagar and would try to inspire as many people as possible.

About The Author

Prakhar Gupta:

He is a modern author born in the 21st century. He predominantly writes inspiring stories conveying life lessons to the audience.

www.ingramcontent.com/pod-product-compliance
Lightning Source LLC
Chambersburg PA
CBHW020519160726
47991CB00007B/3024